Happy Birthday in
DragonWood

Timothy Knapman   Gwen Millward

PUFFIN

Do you think these dragons are scary?

To Ben, who taught the dragons to play football, and to Hamish,
whose birthday it is this year, with love T.K.

To Ianto, Helen and Rhiannon, love G.M.

PUFFIN BOOKS
Published by the Penguin Group: London, New York, Australia, Canada, India, Ireland, New Zealand and South Africa
Penguin Books Ltd, Registered Offices: 80 Strand, London WC2R 0RL, England

puffinbooks.com

Published in Puffin Books 2012
001 – 10 9 8 7 6 5 4 3 2 1
Text copyright © Timothy Knapman, 2012
Illustrations copyright © Gwen Millward, 2012
Made and printed in China

ISBN: 978–0–141–50237–3

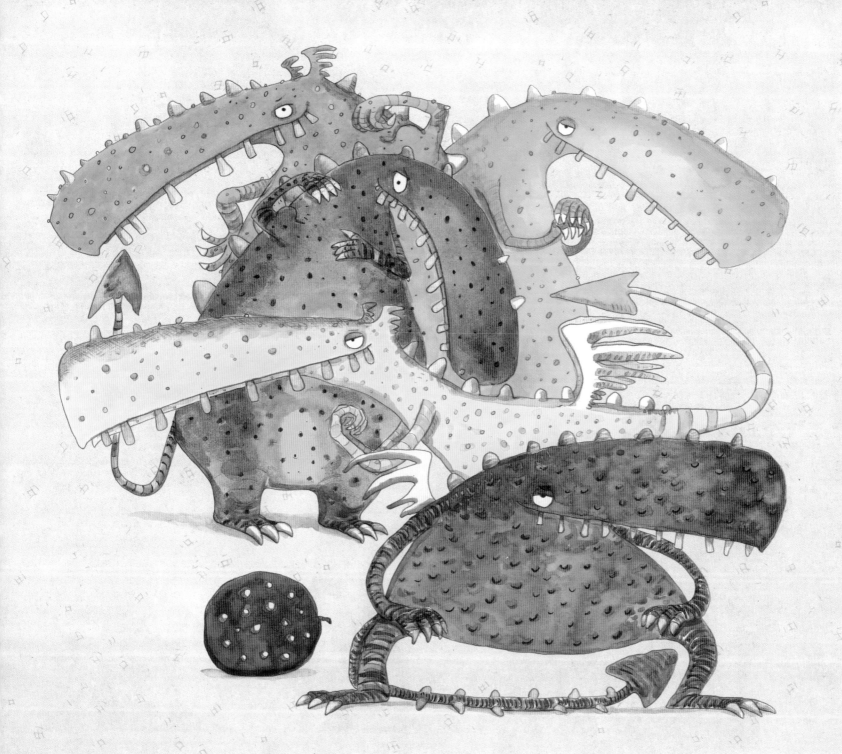

I think they're **scary**,
and **I AM** a dragon.

I have to play football against them,
but I don't stand a chance.
I need a **FRIEND** to help me.

Luckily, I've got one.

He is a thing called a Benjamin.

This is a picture of him.

I know he looks a bit peculiar
but he's my best friend.
He knows EVERYTHING
about football.

But he lives in a magical land far away
so I have to fetch him first.

I'd missed the Benjamin.

He said he'd **love** to help us with our football, but he couldn't stay
for the game itself. Because today was his birthday, you see,
and on their birthdays, Benjamins have a "party".
I didn't know what that was,
so the Benjamin told me.

His friends come round to sing at him
and eat the most DISGUSTING food –
cakes and sweets and ice cream!
Can you imagine it? Yuck!

Little cakes

Bags of air
called balloons

Funniest of all is
that they blow on candles
to put them OUT!

Big cake

Lots of
sugary snacks

I didn't want the Benjamin to miss his party
so we set off **straight away.**

WoO-hoO!

When we got back home, the Benjamin
told us EVERYTHING about football.

You CAN use your wings.

You CAN pass the ball with your tail.

But you CAN'T stuff it down a volcano
and you must NOT set it on fire.

Most important of all:
you'll ONLY win if you help each other.

So much to remember!

He is a VERY good friend.

The game was about to start.
The Benjamin wished us luck and
Dad said he'd give him a lift home.

But as he was hugging me goodbye,

my eyes started leaking – just like the Benjamin's!

That's NEVER happened before.

We helped each other, just like the Benjamin told us to.

We passed the ball with our tails.

We did NOT set it on fire.

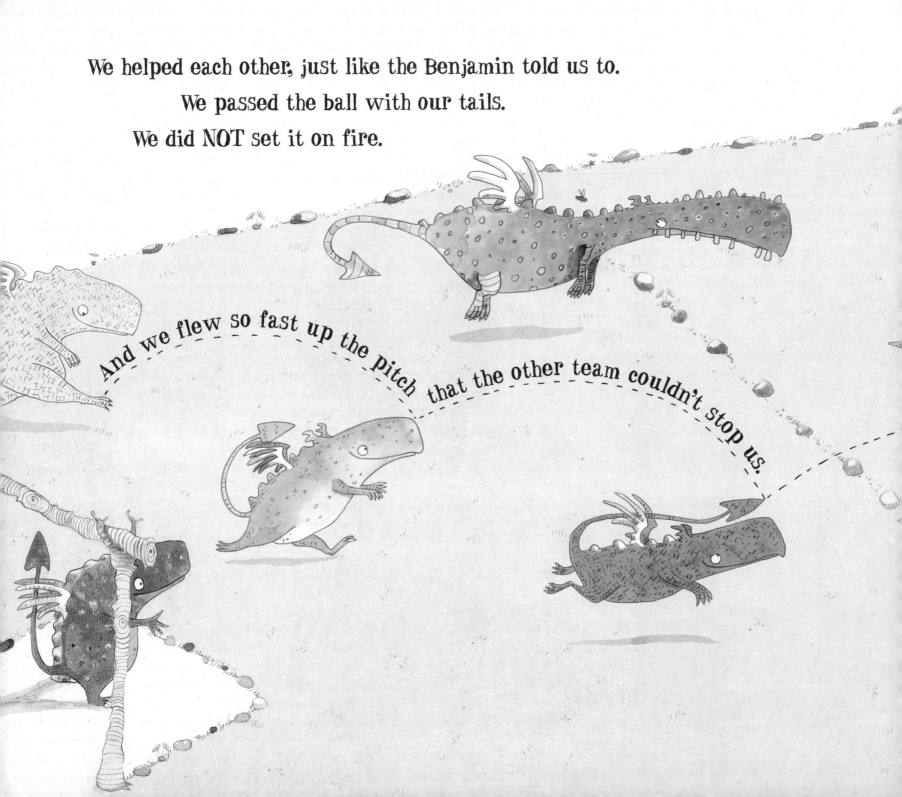

And we flew so fast up the pitch that the other team couldn't stop us.

Goalposts →

Penalty area ↑

All I had to do now was kick the ball
into the net without bursting it
and we'd WIN!

So why did I feel so sad?

Then I heard SOMEONE
cheering me on.

"Come on, Dragon Wood!"

It was ALL I needed.

GOOOOAAL

LL!!

"HOORAY!"

shouted

the Benjamin.

"I thought you had to get back to your friends
and your birthday party," I said.

"I can't have a party without my BEST FRIEND,"
said the Benjamin and he gave me a hug.
"So you'll have to come back with me.

If we hurry

we might just get there in time."

The food was **revolting,**
and the singing
made my **ears hurt.**

But do you know what?

Party
headdress →

← This is called
a "Rover"

← Bunting

← Cake

This is called
a "Felix"

It was even more FUN than football.

I think I might have a birthday party myself
next year. But only if my friend,
the Benjamin, can come.

Though I'll never get the hang of blowing on candles to put them OUT.
NO MATTER HOW MUCH I PRACTISE.

Lots and lots
of tries